TABLE OF CONTENTS

YASMIN

The Teacher

written by
SAADIA FARUQI

illustrated by
HATEM ALY

raintree

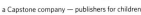
a Capstone company — publishers for children

To Mariam for inspiring me, and
Mubashir for helping me find the
right words—S.F.

To my sister, Eman, and her amazing
girls, Jana and Kenzi—H.A.

Raintree is an imprint of Capstone Global Library Limited, a company
incorporated in England and Wales having its registered office at
264 Banbury Road, Oxford, OX2 7DY – Registered company number:
6695582

www.raintree.co.uk
myorders@raintree.co.uk

Text © Capstone Global Library Limited 2020
The moral rights of the proprietor have been asserted.

Edited by Kristen Mohn
Designed by Lori Bye
Original illustrations © Capstone Global Library Limited 2020
Originated by Capstone Global Library Ltd
Printed and bound in India

ISBN 978 1 4747 6971 6
23 22 21 20 19
10 9 8 7 6 5 4 3 2 1

British Library Cataloguing in Publication Data
A full catalogue record for this book is available from the British
Library.

Acknowledgements
Design elements: Shutterstock: Art and Fashion, rangsan paidaen

CHAPTER 1

A present

Yasmin's Aunt Zara came over to Yasmin's house for tea.

"I have a present for you, jaan!" Aunt Zara said. She handed Yasmin a package.

Yasmin ripped it open.

A box of coloured pencils!

"I love to colour!" Yasmin said.

Then Yasmin noticed a delicious smell. She held the pencils up to her nose. They were scented! Vanilla, strawberry, mango, chocolate!

"Shukriya! Thank you so much!" Yasmin cried. "Please come again with more presents!"

Aunt Zara laughed.

The next day at school,

Yasmin showed her present to

Emma and Ali. "Smell my new

pencils," she said.

Ali took a big sniff.

"Amazing! I wish I had some."

Yasmin was about to say that

Emma and Ali could both choose

a pencil to keep. But then the

bell rang.

CHAPTER 2

Yasmin in charge

During a maths lesson Ms

Alex handed out worksheets.

"Work quietly, please," she said.

The problems were difficult,

but Yasmin could do them.

Counting. Addition. Subtraction.

A knock on the door surprised the children. It was Mr Nguyen, the headmaster. "Ms Alex, can I see you for a minute, please?"

Ms Alex said, "I'm leaving Yasmin in charge. You must all stay as quiet as little mice. And please finish your worksheets!"

She stepped into the corridor and closed the door.

Yasmin couldn't believe she was in charge. She wanted to make Ms Alex proud.

"Hey, everybody!" yelled Ali.

"Watch my cool moves!"

Ali started dancing on the reading mat. The other children giggled.

Emma began to colour on her notepad. "I'm going to draw Yasmin the teacher!" she said loudly.

"Shh!" hissed Yasmin. "We have to be as quiet as little mice."

But everyone just talked and laughed. And nobody did their worksheets.

The class was out

of control!

CHAPTER 3

The scented-pencil solution

Yasmin felt like crying.

What could she do to make

Ms Alex proud?

"Please do your

worksheets!" Yasmin said.

Nobody listened.

Emma had almost finished her picture. "I need pink," she said. "Has anyone got pink?"

That gave Yasmin an idea. The scented pencils! She had plenty to share. She got out her box and waved it in the air.

"How about a competition?" she shouted.

Everyone stopped and looked at her.

"I'll give a scented pencil as a prize to whoever completes the worksheet!" she said.

The children were suddenly as quiet as little mice. They sat back down and worked hard at counting, addition and subtraction.

Ali put up his hand. He needed help. Yasmin showed him how to answer the problem.

"I win!" Ali said as he finished the worksheet.

"Well done!" Yasmin said. "Which pencil would you like?"

Ali chose chocolate. "Thanks, Yasmin!"

Next was Emma. "I'll take strawberry," she said. "Thank you, Yasmin!"

Soon all the children had finished and were quietly drawing with their new pencils.

Ms Alex returned. "Such well-behaved children!" she said. "Yasmin, you've been an excellent teacher today!"

Yasmin grinned. "Thanks, but I'm glad to be one of the class again!"

Think about it, talk about it

* Yasmin feels frustrated when her classmates won't listen to her. Think about a time you felt frustrated. What did you do about it?

* Yasmin has to think creatively to convince her classmates to do their work. If Yasmin hadn't had the coloured pencils, can you think of other possible solutions for her problem?

* It takes courage to be a leader or to try something new. What are some ways that you give yourself courage when you need it?

Learn Urdu with Yasmin!

Yasmin's family speaks both English and Urdu. Urdu is a language from Pakistan. Perhaps you already know some Urdu words!

baba father

hijab scarf covering the hair

jaan life; a sweet nickname for a loved one

mama mother

naan flatbread baked in the oven

nana grandfather on mother's side

nani grandmother on mother's side

salaam hello

shukriya thank you

Pakistan fun facts

Yasmin and her family are proud of their Pakistani culture. Yasmin loves to share facts about Pakistan!

Location

Pakistan is on the continent of Asia, with India on one side and Afghanistan on the other.

Islamabad

PAKISTAN

Education

There are 51 universities and 155,000 primary schools in Pakistan.

First female leader

Benazir Bhutto was the first female Prime Minister of Pakistan, and of any Muslim nation.

Sport

The official sport of Pakistan is hockey.

Make scented pencils!

YOU WILL NEED:

- wooden pencils
- newspaper
- scissors
- sticky tape
- water
- fruit juices such as lemon, lime or orange
- one large bowl (big enough to hold pencils) for each type of juice
- plate

STEPS:

1. Cut out pieces of newspaper wide enough to fit the length of the pencil and long enough to wrap around a few times. Wrap each pencil tightly and use tape to keep the paper in place.

2. Pour water into one bowl and mix in one type of juice. Add enough juice to make a strong scent. Then fill the other bowls with water and one type of juice in each.

3. Put one or more paper-covered pencils into each bowl. Allow to soak for 1 to 3 hours.

4. Take the pencils out and place them on a plate in a sunny place. Allow to sit for 1 to 3 hours.

5. Once the pencils are dry, remove the newspaper. Now your pencils will have scents!

Saadia Faruqi is a Pakistani American
writer, interfaith activist and cultural
sensitivity trainer previously profiled
in *O Magazine*. She is author of the
adult short story collection, *Brick Walls:
Tales of Hope & Courage from Pakistan*.
Her essays have been published in
Huffington Post, Upworthy and *NBC
Asian America*. She lives in Texas, USA,
with her husband and children.

Hatem Aly is an Egyptian-born illustrator whose work has been featured in multiple publications worldwide. He currently lives in New Brunswick, Canada, with his wife, son and more pets than people. When he is not dipping cookies in a cup of tea or staring at blank pieces of paper, he is usually drawing books. One of the books he illustrated is *The Inquisitor's Tale* by Adam Gidwitz, which won a Newbery Honour and other awards, despite Hatem's drawings of a farting dragon, a two-headed cat and stinky cheese.

Join Yasmin
on all her adventures!

Discover more at
www.raintree.co.uk